S.I.L.F. (SANTA I'D LIKE TO F*)

A BBW & BILLIONAIRE BOSS CHRISTMAS ROMANCE

LANA LOVE

LOVE HEART BOOKS

Copyright © 2021 by Lana Love

All rights reserved.

No part of this book may be reproduced in any form or by any electronic or mechanical means, including information storage and retrieval systems, without written permission from the author, except for the use of brief quotations in a book review.

Also by Lana Love
HIS CURVY BEAUTY
The unputdownable series
https://www.amazon.com/gp/product/B07ZSF3TW9

For even more books, please visit my Amazon author page at:

https://www.amazon.com/Lana-Love/e/B078KKRB1T/

❀ Created with Vellum

CHAPTER 1

CHRISSY

"We're giving the promotion to Gayle. I'm so sorry, Chrissy. It was a very tough decision to make, but with the work Gayle did on the recent Gold Ridge Project, she earned the promotion. You do good work. There's a promotion in your future, too."

"But…" I smile to mask my angry frustration. I'd like to say I didn't think she'd do this, but that would be a lie. I expected it. "I just finished my MBA. Does that make a difference?"

"Oh, you finished? That's…good. Congratulations. That was an *online* degree, right?" The way she says "online" is an insult she doesn't even try to hide. Chester University is fully accredited and well regarded, and she knows it.

I nod in response, not trusting myself to say anything.

Deena smiles at me as she flicks her straightened hair, but I know there is nothing but pure poison behind that sickeningly sweet smile. This isn't the first time she's promoted one of her inner circle over me, but the rage building in me demands that it be the last time. If I don't get a promotion soon, recruiters are going to look at my resume and think I

LANA LOVE

do a bad job. Maybe it's time to interview with the company that's been emailing me for months now.

On the face of it, working here at Wade Technical Holdings International is a dream come true. But working for Deena is a nightmare. I'm not even sure why she hired me in the first place, since I don't feed her narcissistic ego the way the other PMs do. Maybe she thought that because I'm fat, I'd be a pushover and kiss her ass just for existing?

"Okay. Thanks for letting me know, Deena."

"Of course." Deena stands and I can't tell if the look that passes over her face is either relief that I didn't cause a scene or regret that she doesn't have grounds to fire me like if I *had* caused a scene. "We can schedule more frequent one-on-one meetings, if you like, so I can review your work and give you pointers for success."

"That would be good. Thank you, Deena. I really do want to succeed here." *And get away from you.* I give her my best smile, though I'm pretty sure she knows it's just as fake as hers.

I return to my tiny office, which is practically a storage closet, and I want to scream. *Don't give her the satisfaction of seeing you upset.* That's what my best friend Frances always says. A glance at the clock confirms it's nearly lunchtime.

Lunch?

Frances replies to my text immediately.

Yes! I can be there in 15.

∼

"Frances, I don't know how much more I can take of this job!" I hate the whining sound of my voice, but I can't help it. "I thought this was going to be the job that launched my career, but now I'm just dealing with mean girls. It's worse than high school! I'm starting to wish I hadn't gotten this job.

S.I.L.F. (SANTA I'D LIKE TO F*)

All they do is give me the grunt work while they get to work on the really interesting parts of a project. It's so unfair!"

Frances motions for the waiter and picks up the wine list.

"Are you sure you don't want wine?"

"I wish." I look longingly at the wine list she's holding, but I know a whiff of alcohol on my breath would be terrible right now. "I'm not like you, babe. My boss wouldn't appreciate it too much if I came back with wine on my breath."

"Well, I'm still having one. My boss is in Europe looking at fabric. I'll have a glass of the prosecco." The waiter nods and looks at me.

"Iced tea, thanks. Extra lemon."

I'm not even sure I should take this long for lunch today, because Deena gave me a bunch of work to do this morning, but there was no way I could stay in the office after our meeting. My head was ready to explode.

"Girl, you should just quit. How long have you been there now? Two years?"

"Nearly two." My voice is quiet. It's embarrassing. "If I stay there any longer without a promotion, it's going to look bad on my resume."

"Why don't you leave now? Isn't that other company still wanting to interview you?"

"Believe me," I say, being sure to keep my voice quiet, "I'd love to. But I'm surprising my grandparents with a trip to Hawaii for their fiftieth wedding anniversary. I've already put a non-refundable deposit down and I'm counting on my Christmas bonus so I can pay off the balance, and then surprise my grandparents. Their anniversary is Valentine's Day."

"I thought you were making good money. Can't you put it on a credit card?" Frances asks, taking a sip of her prosecco.

"Well, I am. But I also have a horrendous mountain of student loan debt. I'm barely keeping my head above water as it is. Putting more on my credit card wouldn't do me any favors. I'm not lucky like you."

Frances is a fashion designer who got lucky and sold her first collection before we'd even graduated from college. She won a prestigious apprenticeship with Mimi de Vrie, who is only the most famous American designer of the last decade.

"You'll have success, too, Chrissy. I got really lucky, and I know it."

"You also work harder than anyone I know. You always have. It'll be your name in Vogue soon."

"You do, too. You deserved that promotion. It sucks so bad that your boss is such a bitch."

The waiter puts my salad in front of me and I just don't feel hungry anymore. Is this really how my career will go? Work my ass off to earn a promotion, and then be denied?

"Let me make you a dress for this holiday party? I can sneak you a Mimi dress."

I roll my eyes at her. This isn't the first time she's offered to make a dress for me, and it probably won't be the last.

"Frances, you know why. Mimi only makes dresses for skinny girls and I," I suck in my stomach and gesture down at my body, "am not skinny. I love you for offering, but I don't think one of her dresses would work on me. I have too much...body. Why would someone want to see a curvy woman like me in one of her dresses, anyway? It's not like she designs dresses for women like me."

"You have a beautiful body," she says, not missing a beat. I've always been overweight, and she's always tried to tell me I'm beautiful. When men look for a beautiful woman, they never seem to look at me. I get men's attention when they find out I'm smart, but they never seem to find me sexy. "People need to see women like you wearing beautiful dresses. I swear I'll make you look amazing."

"Thanks." I know better than to disagree with her. I love her for complimenting me, even if I don't really believe it.

"You're going to call that recruiter, right? Today?"

Frances is giving me a big hug outside my office building. I hug her back tightly, my breath catching a little at how much I love my best friend. She believes in me, even when I'm not sure I believe in myself.

"Yeah, I am." I focus my resolve. I have to do this. No matter how much I fought to get the job at Wade Tech and how much I love the eye candy that is my CEO, Dallas Wade, also known as The Boss I'd Like to Fuck, I know I have to put my career first and chase the better job.

"Remember, the offer of a dress still stands. Plus, you could help my career, too, if you get photographed wearing the dress. Publicity like that will help when I apply for that reality show, Sew It Up."

"But what will Mimi say?"

"Well, she'll have my ass for it and rip me a new one, that's for sure. But if you make it in the society columns and the dress is praised, she'll say it was her idea all along. It's a win-win."

"Hm. Well, I'll think about it." I smile and watch Frances as she hails a cab to take her back to her studio. Maybe I should take her up on the dress. Frances is incredibly talented and the prospect of a fancy ball gown for the Christmas party is appealing.

I enter the lobby to get out of the cold weather and look at my phone. Before I can think too much about it, I call the recruiter who's been calling me for the last three months.

"Hi, Sharlene. This is Chrissy Patton. If that PM position is still available, I'd love to talk."

"Chrissy, can you come into my office?"

I look up at the sound of Mr. Wade's voice and consciously make sure to close my mouth. It's not every day that the boss I've been fantasizing about fucking for nearly two years asks me into his office, much less even knows my name.

So many of my fantasies have involved him inviting me into the office of my CEO, locking the door, and then doing everything HR videos expressly forbid.

Gulping, I nod, then bite my lip when he walks in front of me. His muscles move underneath his fancy suit, and I bite my lip to keep from audibly sighing. I sneak a glance at Deena. Predictably, her face is red with anger and she's glaring at me. I don't know why she's mad at me – *he* asked to talk to *me*.

Mr. Wade gestures toward the couch in his office, then sits in a club chair opposite from me.

I perch on the edge of the couch, my body rigid. He's staring at me with an intensity that makes my insides squirm. I want to pull him over to me, and then ride him until we both can't stand up straight.

"How are things going with the Blue Hills project?" His voice is rich and deep, and it takes every ounce of my self-control to focus on what he's saying and not think about the decidedly HR-unfriendly fantasies crowding my brain.

"Sir, it's—"

"Please," he interrupts, "call me Dallas."

I stare at him for a long moment. This man is famously formal and authoritative. This feels...almost friendly. I'm either getting fired or I'm lost in a delicious dream.

"Well, Dallas," I pause, letting his name linger on my lips, "it's going well. The numbers are looking good, but there are

S.I.L.F. (SANTA I'D LIKE TO F*)

some snags we're working through. Nothing major," I add quickly, "just waiting to get more information so we can finish running some new data models. As far as I know, we're still on schedule. Certainly Deena has told you all this."

Deena has this way of getting everyone to do *her* work, and then taking all the credit. I love working in project management and working on different products and launches, but Deena makes my life miserable. An intern could do all the number-crunching that I do. I want to be the lead Project Manager and talk to clients and make the presentations that sell our products.

"She has," Mr. Wade says slowly, his eyes studying me closely. "But I like to check in with team members from time to time, too, to get their take on things."

That's the first I've heard of that. Since when does a CEO care about what a junior Project Manager thinks?

"Is there a specific question I can answer for you, Dallas?"

"I hear you're now taking over the task of working with a mixologist for the custom cocktail for this year's holiday party. Is that right?"

"That's true, yes." I leave out that the only reason Deena gave me this job is because she got an STD and is on an antibiotic, and her doctor made her swear she wouldn't drink alcohol. I only know this because I overheard her in the bathroom, talking to her friend. To my face, she made some excuse about a last-minute project that Mr. Wade asked her to work on, and then made it sound like some grand gift she was bestowing on me

"Good." Mr. Wade smiles and I can't help but gasp at how happy he looks about this. I've been dreading this project because it's just more of her work that Deena wants me to do. It's not a bad project, but given that I'm not even sure I want to go to the company Christmas party, it feels like a big F U that I have to choose a signature drink for the event. "I have a free evening and I'm going to come with you."

This time, I can't control myself and my mouth hangs open. I've fantasized about spending evenings with Mr. Wade – especially naked – but I never imagined it would happen!

"You're what?"

CHAPTER 2

DALLAS

Seeing Chrissy squirm on my couch makes my cock throb with raging desire. I want to see her squirming, without a stitch of clothing on her stunning body, and preferably while she's riding my cock and screaming my name.

But for now, I have to be satisfied with how she looks in her blue dress.

"Um, are you sure about this? This doesn't seem like the kind of thing that you'd be involved in."

Deena recommended one of her friends to take over for her on the signature drink selection, but I knew that Chrissy was the better choice. Deena likes to think that I don't pay that close of attention to the individual members of her team, but I do. Deena does a good job, but I also know she plays favorites.

"Well, I'm the boss. I say it's okay." I smile at her, savoring the way she blushes. She may think I haven't noticed how she looks at me with naked longing, but she's wrong. From the moment I laid eyes on her, I paid attention to her. I've followed the work she's done and she's smart. Brains and a glorious body? She's my dream girl.

"I didn't know that you were involved in the party planning."

"Normally I'm not," I say, stretching my legs in front of me. A spark of satisfaction rises when I see how her eyes focus on my legs and how she swallows as if she's hiding great emotion. She catches herself and returns to her professional demeanor, but not before licking her red lips. Fuck. I need to taste those lips. "I thought it would be an amusing diversion."

"O-okay. What do you have in mind?" Her eyes flare as she tilts her head at me. She's watching me carefully and it's obvious there's a lot going on in her pretty head. The spark of ambition is clear in her eyes, but there's also hesitancy. It's the hesitancy that is surprising. In its way, it's refreshing, because it means I actually have to work to win her over – and I welcome a challenge. It's boring when people just say yes.

And when you have as much money and power as I do, *everyone* says yes to you.

"This year," I say, leaning forward, my legs spread apart, "I want to be more involved. Be more hands-on, as they say."

My cock twitches as I watch the blush that spreads from her neck to her chest, and then under the top of her blouse. *Oh, this is going to be fun.*

"Of course, Dallas." She begins regaining her composure and I admire her resilience. "Have you, um, done this kind of thing before?"

"No," I laugh. "I've always hired people to do that."

The truth is, I've been watching her for quite a while, and organizing this Christmas party was a way to be close to her and see if she's even half the woman that I think she is.

"Excuse me," I say when my phone buzzes. "Yes? What?

S.I.L.F. (SANTA I'D LIKE TO F*)

I'm on my way." Turning back to Chrissy, I'm genuinely sorry to have to part from her. "I apologize. Duty calls."

"Of course. I'll prepare a list of ideas and send them over to you."

I look at her full lips, desire building inside of me. The urge to kiss her lips is blinding, but I can't. No matter how much I don't want to, I have to keep this professional. The VP of HR would go nuclear on my ass if she knew I was even considering touching Chrissy. But how am I supposed to resist a plump cutie with the most vibrant red hair that I've ever seen?

"Excellent. I'll be in touch."

~

"As you can see, we're going to miss projections if we don't make some changes." Julian's voice is shaky. He has every reason to be scared. This project is already behind schedule and over-budget.

I flip through the report in front of me. The numbers swim in front of my eyes, my brain not paying attention. There's a reason I pay other people to attend meetings like this. But when one of my Senior VPs requests my presence, I attend.

"Julian. You need to fix this yesterday. What do you need me for?"

Julian's eyes cut away at the harshness of my voice.

"Sir, we'd like your authorization to…restructure this project. Infuse some new money into it. If you flip to page nine of the report," he pauses, "you'll see that we want to bring in some new talent, probably from Grayson Technology. Fresh eyes will help us spot what's bogging us down. They have a stellar reputation."

"Fine. Do it." I close the report and push it into the middle of the table. "Is there anything else?"

My eyes move around the team seated at the table. No one meets my eyes, except Julian, who still looks like he's shaking.

"Thank you for your vote of confidence. We'll give you an update next Friday."

I push my chair out from the table and stride out of the conference room. I need to be alone.

Ever since my meeting with Chrissy, she's been all I can think about. Returning to my office, I tell my assistant not to disturb me.

I stare out the window to the busy city streets fifty floors below, watching the unending movement of the world. My email pings and my cock twitches when I see it's an email from Chrissy. Scanning over her ideas, I smile, then email her. I have an idea of my own.

Meet me in the lobby at 6.

CHAPTER 3

CHRISSY

"You're early. Good."

I jump at the sound of my boss' voice and nearly drop my phone on the marble floor of the lobby. Frances has been urging me to make a pass at him, convinced that he must want curvy me simply because he requested I meet with him. Having earthshatteringly hot sex with the CEO of my company is a sexy fantasy, but that's not how things work in my life. I'm always the quiet mouse toiling away.

"What are we working on? Your message earlier was...cryptic."

"Drinks."

"Pardon me?" I look at Dallas, confused. His eyes meet mine and it's an electric jolt through my body. When Dallas looks at me, it feels like he actually sees me and wants to be with me.

Is this...is this a *date*? But how is that even possible? I chide myself and my overactive – and highly sexed – imagination. Why would he want to go on a date with me? He's my boss' boss—I'm still shocked that he knows my *name*.

LANA LOVE

"Thank you for sending the list of mixologists you were considering. I've pulled a few strings and have lined up someone new."

A flash of anger flares in me. I start to open my mouth, then close it. If I could, I'd just quit this job now, no matter how sexy Dallas is and how much just a glance from him makes me want to jump on him and have the kind of sex that makes you question whether your body can handle that much lusty pleasure.

"I looked over your list of suggestions. Those mixologists were good, but I have one I want you to try. If you don't like her, then you can choose the next one. Deal?" Without waiting for a response, Dallas puts his hand on the small of my back and guides me through the lobby and toward the elevator bank. I have to stop myself from pushing into his fingers, like a cat demanding attention. I imagine his fingers trailing over my bare skin, slowly exploring me, then his fingers opening me between my legs, stroking me faster and faster until I forget my name. "My driver is already waiting outside."

With his hand on my back, I have a moment of feeling special. But I'm more confused than anything else.

"I don't want to sound impertinent, but don't you have... better things to do? This doesn't seem like something you'd be involved in."

Dallas' green eyes pierce mine and my heart burns with desire. He's totally out of my league, but he's everything I want in a man. He built his empire from nothing, he's intelligent, and he's sexy as sin. He's also famously single and private, which is perhaps not the best man to daydream about.

"Honestly, I thought it would be a nice change of pace from the endless meetings I normally face each day." He sighs as he smooths his hands over his legs. I'm not sure I fully believe him, but getting to spend time with the man who is sexier than any man I've ever laid eyes on? It's not something I'm going to say no to. "Plus, I get to spend time with you."

I'm not sure why he's acting like a normal guy and treating me like someone he cares about, but for tonight, I'm going to enjoy it. It always seemed like he's just as cold as Deena, which is part of why I accepted the interview at King Technical Ventures. I've only stayed this long at this job because I need my holiday bonus.

But now? He's showing an interest in me and…wants to be with me. Is this some kind of joke? It doesn't feel like a pity date, but my track record with men isn't great…so what do I know?

The driver pulls up at the curb of The Maxwell Arms, one of the swankest bars in town. Getting their award-winning mixologist bartender to craft a custom cocktail for the party was my biggest stretch goal. I couldn't even get Ursula Young to return any of my emails or phone calls. I'd bet a lot of money that the only reason that we're here is because it sounds like Dallas made the call personally. And everyone knows a man as rich and famous as Dallas Wade gets everything he wants.

Inside, the hostess stares at Dallas before leading us to a private room. There is a tall, flocked Christmas tree next to a floor-to-ceiling window and because The Maxwell Arms sits on top of Aster Hill, the city is laid at our feet. The city below us looks like a fairy tale, twinkling lights contrasting against the ink-darkness of the sky.

"Hello, Mr. Wade. Pleasure to see you again."

I turn and see a tall woman with tattoos covering her muscular arms. She's wearing a sleeveless black dress, with a starched white apron around her waist.

"Ursula. A pleasure, as always. What do you have for us this evening?"

Ursula motions to a table by the window, and then gets to work behind a small bar.

"Well, you didn't give much notice, but I have a few ideas."

What follows is the most amazing bar experience I've ever had. She creates a series of drinks as she talks to us, letting us taste each so we can choose one. Originally, I thought having a signature drink for the Christmas party was pretentious, but now that I'm sitting in front of the best mixologist in the city, with the sexiest man in the city next to me, I'm rethinking that. This is luxury defined and I hadn't even realized cocktails could taste this good. Between the delicious drinks and Dallas' thigh pressing against mine and lighting my body like a Christmas tree, this is the best Wednesday night I've ever had.

"Okay. You two have a chat, then let me know which you prefer. Take your time. If you'd like to order food, just press the call button." Ursula gestures toward a discreet intercom by the door, then nods and departs.

"Are you hungry?"

I look toward the menus that Ursula placed on the table and my stomach rumbles.

"I'll take that as a yes." The sound of Dallas chuckling unexpectedly puts me at ease. After he's ordered dinner for both of us, he slides into the booth and sits so close to me I can smell a hint of his cologne. The earthy, musky scent of his cologne makes me want to rub my body against his, so that I'm marked by his scent.

"You smell good." I clap my hand over my mouth as soon as I realize I said what I was thinking out loud. *Those drinks were stronger than I thought.* Despite just taking sips of all the drinks Ursula made, the booze has gone straight to my head.

"Thank you, Chrissy." There's a smile on his face, but the look in Dallas' eyes changes and it goes deep inside of me. It sounds corny, but it feels like he's looking into my soul.

When he leans closer to me, I can't stop the moan that comes out of me when I feel his hot breath on my neck. He's not even touching me, but the closeness of his body is intoxicating.

"This feels dangerous." My voice is a whisper, but I don't move away. I know all the reasons this is wrong. Even if it's just for a few weeks longer, this man is my boss. *But if I'm quitting soon? Why can't I have some fun?*

Dallas gently pushes my hair back and brushes his lips against my ear. My core flares with a flame of desire and I clench my thighs together.

"Do you really want to be *safe*?"

I turn my head to look at Dallas and I can't resist myself. I move my head slightly and before I can even blink, his mouth and lips are hot against mine, igniting a bonfire of raw lust in me.

Dallas' lips are firm against mine and his tongue dominates my mouth. He tastes like the delicious cocktails we've been drinking and I tease his tongue with mine, hungry for him.

A frustrated moan comes out of my lips when he pulls his mouth from mine. I don't want this to be over.

But when I look at him, the hunger in his green eyes makes me shiver. He's looking at me with a passion that I've never experienced. In his eyes, I feel worthy of a man like him.

"I want to taste you." His voice is thick and husky, and then his mouth is back on mine. I lean back and welcome his strong tongue in my mouth again, squirming in my seat at how hot and wet I'm getting. *I need to get out of here and have a date with my vibrator...*

The firm touch of his fingers on my leg tickles and I squirm as he pushes my dress up my thighs, his fingers teasing against my skin.

Oh my God! Is this really happening?

My mind starts racing as his fingers get closer to my core. I know that sleeping with your boss is a million kinds of wrong, but I throw it all to the wind and kiss him more deeply, spreading my legs for him and inviting him to touch me. I tell my overactive brain to shut up, because it's been way too long since a man looked at me. If I have a chance to spend a night with my sexy boss, then I'm damn well going to say yes!

"Take off your pantyhose."

My knees wobble as I kick off my heels and stand in front of him. I bunch the fabric of my dress in my hands, then shimmy out of my tights. A fire burns in Dallas' eyes as he watches me and I see his fingers flexing.

All at once, a skin-tingling rush of emotion overtakes me. Dallas is looking at me with naked, fierce lust and it makes my heart race. One of the richest men in the world is staring at me like I'm the most desirable woman in the universe, and I can't help but feel sexy and powerful.

"How do you want me?" I sway my hips as I look at Dallas.

"Sit on my lap."

I step up to him and straddle his lap. Dallas immediately puts his hands on my ass and moves me closer to him. My breasts push against his chest and I can feel his heart pounding. My mouth finds his and I grind on his lap as he holds me tight against his body.

When his fingers push into my panties and slide between my slick folds, I tilt my head back and moan. His fingertip is light against my clit, circling it and teasing it. My body takes over and presses into his hand, desperate to have his fingers stroking inside of me.

Finally, he slides his fingers into me and I push down, my breathing jagged as he strokes the most inner, private part of me. His fingers probe my inner walls and my hips work faster, my orgasm building deep inside of me.

But before I can come, he slides his fingers out of me.

"What?" I can't even see straight because my body is so electrified by the firm stroke of his fingers. Why did he stop?

"I wanted to see how you taste..." Dallas smiles broadly at me, then he slowly puts his index finger in his mouth and sucks it. His eyelids flutter with pleasure and it turns me on even more to watch him taste me like this. "You are even more delicious than I imagined, Chrissy."

Before I can say anything, there's a discreet knocking at the door to our private room. I glance at the door and back at Dallas, not fully comprehending what's happening. But Dallas just keeps smiling at me and licking his other finger clean.

"You should take a seat. Our dinner has arrived."

CHAPTER 4

DALLAS

It doesn't take an HR manager to tell me that what happened last night was dangerous. But fuck almighty, it was worth it. Teasing her as she straddled my lap and rode my fingers? It was the most erotic thing I've experienced in far too long. She gave herself to me with an abandon that took my breath away. And fuck. I lick my lips just remembering the delicious tang of her juices as I licked my fingers clean. I want to spend hours between her legs, eating her sweet pussy.

It was a horrible tease to interrupt our moment, because I wanted to fuck her beautiful brains out, but I wanted to draw out the seduction.

More than anything, I know she has to be mine.

I make my way through the office, ignoring everyone. There is only one person I want to talk to and I'm hoping that she wants to talk to me, too.

"Deena, is Chrissy in?"

Deena looks at me like I'm speaking Greek, then stares at me.

"Is there something I can help you with, sir?" She sits up a

S.I.L.F. (SANTA I'D LIKE TO F*)

little straighter and pushes out her chest, but it does nothing for me. She may think she's subtle about it, but I've known for months that she wants me.

But I don't like starved women and I don't date employees. Well, not until Chrissy.

Chrissy is special. I will do anything for Chrissy.

"No. Please find Chrissy and have her come in to see me."

I turn and walk into my office, not wanting to look at Deena a second longer. I place the bag of food I've been carrying on my desk. I'm starving, but I won't eat until Chrissy joins me or tells me to fuck off.

"You asked to see me?"

Chrissy stands at my door, a wary look in her eyes. The sight of her makes my heart pound in my chest, but the fact she looks scared hurts my heart.

"Chrissy, please come in. Close the door behind you."

She pauses and stares at me, then obeys. As she walks closer to me, I see her nose twitch and her eyes flare.

I rip open the bag and gesture for her to sit.

Chrissy meets my eyes and I'm captivated by the vulnerability and strength in them.

"Well, if you're asking about the cocktails," she smiles, her blue eyes brightening, "then I think that red-colored vodka cocktail, or whatever was in that, was super tasty. That's the kind of drink that you don't care about the hangover you get – and I've definitely got one."

"I wondered if you might. My head protested this morning when my alarm went off. That's why I brought these," I say, nodding to the coffee and greasy breakfast sandwiches.

"You are an angel of mercy." She picks up a breakfast sandwich and takes a huge bite. I love a woman with an appetite and who doesn't deny herself what she wants and what we all know tastes like manna when you have a hangover. After her first bite, she leans back in her chair, her eyes partially closed in ecstasy. It makes me hard again just to watch how she's giving herself over to pleasure with abandon. Before you talk to her, she seems like a quiet and studious woman; but there's an intelligent and deeply sensual woman underneath.

"I'm glad you liked my suggestion of mixologist. You didn't seem that pleased when I changed the plans."

Chrissy looks at me, her eyes wide in alarm. "Was it that obvious? I'm sorry."

I laugh. "A little. I get that I was coming in on your assignment."

Chrissy smiles, taking a drink of the coffee and eating more of the sandwich. I can see them working their magic. Grease and caffeine after a night of drinking always take the edge off and bring you closer to feeling alive again.

"It's okay," she says, though the slight crease of her eyes indicates that maybe it wasn't. "It turned out alright."

"Just alright?" I lean forward and put my elbows on my knees, my eyes drinking in her in. She squirms a little in her chair and instantly I know she wants more of what I started last night, which is good, because I want to make her come every night for the rest of our lives.

"Is it bad if I say I enjoyed it? A lot?"

There's a spark of bravery in her eyes and she licks her lips and takes a bite of her breakfast sandwich. Fuck. This woman is going to do me in. Chrissy isn't like other women. Other women throw themselves at me, looking for a sugar daddy to set them up for life. Chrissy...Chrissy doesn't have that pretense or calculation. It feels like she's interested in *me*, not just my money or power.

"It's not bad. It's what I want to hear."

I close the distance between us and pull her into a kiss. The taste of her lips and tongue unlocks my passion again, and in this moment, there is nothing but her and me. My desire for her is consuming me. If I can't have her, I'm going to go crazy.

Chrissy's hands grasp me and find my hips, and I push into her hands. When she reaches behind me and grabs my ass, I grind into her. Lust has burned away my hangover, and my body is screaming to make her mine.

"Is the door locked?" Chrissy's voice is breathless and her mouth is parted as she looks up at me, desire blatant in her blue eyes.

"It will be."

I freeze five feet from my door. The distinctive rap of Deena's knock cuts through the room. The door starts to open and anger rushes through my body. She knows better than to open my door when it's closed. This is a deliberate act of invasion.

"Sorry to interrupt, Mr. Wade."

"What is it?" My voice is a harsh bark, but I don't care. Deena knows better than to interrupt me when my door is closed. If I hadn't realized how jealous she is of Chrissy, I do now. Deena has been hounding me all morning, practically begging for attention.

"It's the Bull Hills project. I have a contract?"

Fuck. This actually is important, but it doesn't negate her breach of privacy. I watch her gaze slide past me to Chrissy, a smirk of a smile curling on Deena's face. After this contract is signed and sealed, we're going to have a talk about this.

"I'll touch base with you this afternoon," Chrissy says gracefully. I turn and see her standing up, her fingers wrapped around the large coffee I brought. Fuck. I want her fingers around my cock. I stare at her in awe when I see how she's masking the raw desire from a minute ago. She understands discretion. I'm not some achievement for her to brag about. "Thank you for breakfast."

"Good. I'll expect to hear from you this afternoon."

∼

I MIGHT DIE if I don't get out of this meeting.

Blue Hills is a pet project of mine, but right now, all I can think about is Chrissy. I wish it was her with me right now. The sound of city traffic is just detectable through the floor-to-ceiling window behind me. I place my hands on the conference table, my cock growing hard as I imagine Chrissy sitting on the edge of the table, facing me, spreading her legs so that only I can see her sweet pussy.

I imagine kneeling in front of Chrissy, closing my eyes and inhaling her deliciously primal musk. How would she react with my head between her legs, my tongue savoring her slick taste and teasing at her clit? Would she run her fingers through my hair and hold my head where she wants it? Would she lay back and moan as I devoured her pussy? Would she giggle and squirm?

God. I hope she giggles and squirms.

CHAPTER 5

CHRISSY

"Sweetie, I'm so glad you called! I pulled a couple of Mimi's dresses and I'm going to tailor the one you like best so that it fits you like a glove. You're going to be wearing a dress from next season and there is exactly zero chance anyone else will have the same dress."

Frances is standing in reception, a huge garment bag slung over her shoulder. She's looking at me with so much excitement in her eyes, that it stills me. She's my best friend, but there are moments when we're together and my heart expands so much that I don't know how my body can contain it.

"Have I told you lately I love you? Because I do." I give her a big hug and gesture toward the hallway to the conference room I booked. My office is barely big enough for me to have someone sit and talk, and it's certainly not big enough for me to try on dresses and have her take my measurements.

Frances smiles and waves her hand as we walk. I know she has a lot riding on this, too.

Closing the door and pulling the blinds down, I turn to her. "Okay, hotshot. Show me what you're thinking."

"Right. Here are four dresses. I want you to try them on and tell me what you think. I'll take photos and your measurements, and then I'll do my design magic."

"Are you sure you have enough time to do this? Doesn't this kind of thing take ages?" There's a part of me that doesn't believe I can be so lucky as to have a beautiful dress like the one Frances is offering, like maybe it won't work out.

"Absolutely!" Frances' eyes are bright. "Besides, this is good practice for if I make it on Sew It Up."

"When," I correct, smiling at her.

"Fine, *when*. I'll be expected to design and produce a full dress in less time than we have now. This will be a cakewalk."

Frances pulls the dresses out of the bag and I gasp. They're silky and form-fitting. She's brought two black dresses, one of which is so strappy I have no idea how I could wear a bra or panties underneath it. One is an emerald green, but with my red hair I would look terrible.

I bite my lip as I look at the final dress. It's a deep red silk, strappy but not too strappy on the top, and only comes to mid-thigh at best. This is easily the most beautiful dress I have ever been in the presence of and I know it's the only one I even want to try on.

"That one. That's what I want." I walk in front of the dress and look at it lovingly. I'm nearly scared to touch it, because it's so beautiful.

"Hm. That's a bold choice."

"It's so beautiful." Staring at this dress is better than chocolate. The fabric flows and it looks like it would hug my curves perfectly, while also camouflaging the bumps of my stomach. "This is the only dress I want."

"Then your wish is my command. Try it on so I can see how it looks, and then I'll take your measurements so I can adjust it."

I try to step into the dress, but it's way too small for me.

S.I.L.F. (SANTA I'D LIKE TO F*)

Instead, I hold the dress against my body and Frances takes some photos on her phone.

"Oooh. You're right!"

The way Frances is looking at me tells me all I need to know. Her eyes are filled with awe and excitement. She takes a few photos, then a series of measurements.

"Is there anything you want to change?"

"Nothing except the fit, but I know you'll ace that." I smooth my hands over the red silk, the luxury of the fabric against my skin makes me smile. Even without seeing myself in a mirror, this dress just feels right. "Actually, maybe make it longer? Like full length? I want to feel like a princess.

"Alright then. I'll take it home and get to work. The only thing," Frances says, putting down her iPad as she turns to look at me, "is that you have to return it by midnight."

"No problem."

"I don't know why the door is closed. We can meet in here," Deena says as she shoves the door open. "What the...?" Surprise flashes in Deena's eyes, then she smirks when she sees me blushing and holding the dress against my body.

I freeze like a deer in headlights, my hands pressing the front of the dress against my chest. "I reserved this room until two o'clock." I try to stand my ground, but with the amount of skin I'm showing and the fact that I'm not dressed, I feel as powerful as a wet kitten.

"Oh, so sorry. Mr. Wade," she says, turning to our boss. "Shall we talk in your office instead?"

My eyes meet his and my body burns. The raw hunger in his gaze makes me instinctively press my legs together. I know I should look away, but I can't. The intensity of his stare makes me feel like I'm about to go up in flames.

"Of course." Dallas gestures for Deena to leave the conference room. He turns, his eyes raking over my body. "Chrissy?"

"Sir?" I can't help the formality that comes out of my mouth, but I smile when he raises an eyebrow at me saying 'sir.' He tilts his head and I walk over to him, acutely aware that I'm holding a strapless dress against my body.

"This is not a dressing room. If you'd like to take off your clothes while at work…" Dallas lowers his voice and leans his head so that his mouth is next to my ear, "come to my office."

My insides contract and my clit throbs with desire. Dallas doesn't raise his head from mine and his breath is hot against my skin. Each puff of his breath makes me squirm and ache to push myself against his mouth, to feel his tongue lavishing attention on my skin. I'd love nothing more than to drop my dress to the ground, jump on him, and feel his hard cock sink into the hot core of me. It's all sorts of wrong – doing whatever it is we're doing – just like him flirting with me is taboo.

But I love it.

After several long seconds, he steps back from me, then leaves without even acknowledging Frances, who is standing there with her mouth hanging open.

"It's him, isn't it? *That* is 'Boss I'd Like to Fuck'?"

"It's obvious, huh?" I rush to the door and lock it, then carefully hang up the dress and give it back to Frances. "Don't say anything, though."

"My lips are sealed." She smiles and mimes zipping her lips together, and it helps to break the tension in the room. "I'm going to make you look like a million bucks and he won't be able to resist you. Just seriously remember to get the dress back by midnight, because Mimi comes back from her European shopping trip that night and she always goes straight to the studio. If we're lucky, she won't immediately realize it's been altered, before I can change it back to her design; but she'd notice immediately if it wasn't there."

S.I.L.F. (SANTA I'D LIKE TO F*)

After Frances leaves, I camp out in my office and focus on nothing but work. It's only after I finish reconciling yet another spreadsheet that I let myself think about what happened.

Dallas was transfixed when he saw me. I hadn't been sure about what happened between us at The Maxwell Arms, but the way he spoke to me and the way he just…breathed on me? It was fucking hot and it makes me wet – again – to remember how erotic it was. Usually, men can't keep their hands off women, but Dallas restrains himself and the anticipation is hotter than anything I've experienced.

But how does an overweight girl like me fit in with a freaking billionaire?

My phone buzzes and adrenaline spikes when I see the phone number.

"Hello, Chrissy. This is Sharlene from King Technical Ventures. Do you have a minute?"

"Of course, Sharlene." I quietly go to my door and lock it, then triple-check that it's locked. I can't have anyone walking in right now. "What can I do for you? Do you have more questions for me?"

"Actually," she chuckles, "I don't have any further questions. I'll get straight to the point. Everyone loved you. You're bright and intelligent, and Cindy Orangefield would love for you to join her team. Take time to consider our offer, but…"

"I accept!" I could just jump out of my skin with how excited I am. "Thank you so much!"

"That's wonderful news, Chrissy. Cindy will be pleased to hear about your enthusiasm. When are you available to start?"

"I can start in three weeks." On the spur of the moment, I decide to give myself the best birthday gift and take a short vacation before starting my new job.

"That's perfect, Chrissy. We're thrilled to be adding you to our team. I'll email you the contract and all the paperwork, so you can get a headstart on reading through those. Contact me with any questions."

I end the call and pump my arm in the air. I did it! I got a job as a full Project Manager! I can't wait to tell Frances!

But what about Dallas? I'm not sure exactly why, but accepting this new job feels like a betrayal to him. Sure, there's lust between us, but does that mean I have to keep this job? If I leave this job, will…whatever this is between us continue? There's something fiery when we're together, but I don't understand what it *is*. When we're together, it feels like he sees me in a way that men usually don't see me. He treats me like I'm sexy and desirable, not just the fat friend to be polite to.

I press my hands flat on my desk and breathe deeply, trying to calm my heart rate.

I don't know what to do with Dallas.

CHAPTER 6

DALLAS

My heart stops when I see Chrissy. The band is playing Christmas standards, the sound of people laughing and celebrating. All of it disappears. The moment Chrissy arrives, her beauty is breathtaking.

"Excuse me." I extract myself from a conversation that I haven't even been listening to because I've been too distracted searching the crowd, waiting for Chrissy to appear.

"Can I speak with you?" Deena asks.

"Talk to me next week."

"But Mr. Wade…"

I keep walking. Not even caring that I'm being rude to Deena. There is only one person that is important right now. And that is Chrissy.

"You look stunning."

Chrissy looks at me, her blue eyes wide and a shy smile playing on her lips as a blush rises up her cheeks. "Thank you, Dallas."

The band finishes the song they're playing and I formally

reach my hand out toward her. "Would you do me the honor of dancing with me?"

She puts her soft hand into mine and allows me to lead her into the center of the dance floor. By luck, the band begins to play a slower song. Chrissy's soft curves feel delicious and my mind races ahead, anticipating how her naked curves will feel against my naked body.

Chrissy is the only Christmas present that I want this year. I spin her around and the silky feel of her hair brushing against my jaw makes my blood roar with desire. When she spins back to me, I hold her even closer to my body, pressing my hips against her.

"You have some nice moves there, Chrissy."

"You're not so bad yourself, Dallas. I didn't know that you could dance."

"I love moving my body with you, Chrissy." I smile at her, loving that she's blushing again. My passion for her just grows, knowing that she can't hide her reactions from me. Her shyness makes her all the more irresistible. I can't fucking live without her.

It's a delicious game, seeing just how much I can tease her and make her blush. All I can think about is removing this beautiful red dress from her body, exploring her curves, and making love to her. But first, I want to claim my future wife.

"The way you're dancing with me, Dallas, it feels dangerous..." Chrissy's eyes are bright with desire. And I can see that she's teasing me.

"If you want me to stop..." I grin at her and move my arm so that there is space between us.

"No!" she exclaims. "I didn't say that I didn't like it!"

A fast song begins and nothing else in the world exists as Chrissy giggles while I spin her across the dance floor. She dances with an abandon that speaks to my soul. I want to explore this side of her, learn what she likes and then devote myself to giving her every pleasure.

In a flash, her face crumples and she collapses into my arms. I immediately pull her close to me, my hand instinctively rubbing her back to comfort her.

"Chrissy, darling. What's wrong?" I take her weight and guide her off the dance floor and toward a sofa on the edge of the ballroom.

"One of my heels broke. I twisted my ankle."

After I help her sit down comfortably, I sit next to her and lift her feet onto my lap. One of her heels has, indeed, broken and is hanging off. I slip the shoe from her foot and gently massage her ankle, watching her intently to discover the severity of her injury. Confident that her foot isn't broken, I continue massaging her ankle and enjoying the feel of her soft flesh under my strong fingers. I slip off her other shoe and pay attention to that foot.

"That feels divine." Chrissy's voice is breathless, her face completely relaxed. For maybe the first time, her walls are completely gone. She is vulnerable and utterly open, and she's never been more beautiful.

"Drink, sir? Ma'am?"

We both look up to see a waiter in black and white, holding a tray of the Mistletoe Magic cocktail that we chose after our tasting at The Maxwell Arms.

"Yes, please." I raise a glass to Chrissy to toast her. "Thank you for letting me join you that night. I hope you didn't mind too much."

As I hoped, her blush is almost as bright as the red of her dress. She momentarily looks away, a shy smile on her full lips. Every time I think I've never seen a woman look so sexy, she reveals more of herself. She has an allure and beauty I never imagined I would find in a woman. After decades of dating countless women, they always came up short. But

Chrissy? She has an effortless passion that makes her utterly irresistible.

"The pleasure was all mine." Chrissy meets my eyes and sips her drink, and my heart surges with obsession for her.

Staring deeply into her blue eyes, I run my fingers up her leg, under the fullness of her silk dress. She bites her lip as she watches me, her legs pressing together slightly. I arch my eyebrow at her, confused. "Do you want me to stop?"

"No!" Her response is immediate and forceful. "It's just," she glances at the ballroom, which I'd honestly forgotten about, "we're not alone."

"That is an incredibly easy problem to solve." I stand and extend my hand out to her. She smiles as she stands next to me, her eyes shimmering with happiness. Her eyes fall to my watch and the color drains from her face.

"What time is it?"

"It's," I look at my Patek Phillipe watch, "half-past eleven."

"Oh my God! I'm sorry, but I have to go!"

"What? Why on earth…?"

With a truly regretful look on her face, she carefully lifts the full skirt of her dress, limps across the dance floor, and exits the ballroom.

And with that, she's gone. All that I have left are her shoes.

CHAPTER 7

CHRISSY

"Hurry!" I urge the Uber driver to move faster through the streets of downtown. I type a quick text to Frances.

On my way.

The driver looks at me in the rear-view mirror and raises his eyebrow.

"Late for a party?"

"Something like that."

When we finally arrive at the building where Mimi's fashion house is located, I launch myself out of the car before he even comes to a complete stop. I stumble as fast as I can with my sprained ankle, crossing my fingers that there isn't broken glass (or worse) on the ground.

Frances is pacing in the lobby when I arrive.

"I was wondering if you were going to make it." I can tell she's trying to make a joke, but she keeps glancing over her shoulder and her eyes are creased with worry.

"Sorry. Traffic. Who knew the streets would be jammed this late at night?"

"Was it worth it?" Frances smiles at me.

I grin. "Yeah, it was. He loved the dress." I remember how Dallas ran his finger under the shoulder strap of my dress. That simple caress lit a fire in my core. My skin tingles just remembering how it felt to dance in his arms.

Dallas looked more handsome in his tux than a movie star. So many people were watching us and I know everyone was surprised that he spent most of his time with me. Deena didn't bother him, but I saw her a few times and if looks could kill, I'd be dead ten times.

But nothing has ever felt as good as being in Dallas' arms. I fit perfectly, like that's where I belong. When his fingers brushed my bare skin, my body lit up in ways I never thought possible. I always believed that being sexy and desired was something for other women, that I'd never feel that way myself.

I shimmy out of the dress and pull on my leggings and college hoodie. Once again, I feel like I normally do, comfortable and invisible.

"Hey, do you have a pair of shoes I could borrow? Like sneakers? Even flip flops."

"What?" Frances' voice raises in alarm as she looks to my feet and sees how dirty they are. "What happened to your shoes? You spent a fortune on them!"

"One of the heels broke while I was dancing, and I twisted my ankle a little. Dallas was really kind and escorted me off the dance floor, then massaged my ankle and foot."

"He what?" Frances looks at me, her green eyes widening. Then she laughs and shakes her head. "You know he's hot for you, right? Men just don't do that for women they don't care about."

I blush and look away. My heart tells me that she's right, but my head tells me that she's wrong. What on earth does he see in me? Billionaires don't date women with curves.

"Maybe," I finally concede, putting my hands in the

S.I.L.F. (SANTA I'D LIKE TO F*)

hoodie pocket and pushing down. "But he won't like me when I give notice next week."

"He'd be a fool to let you get away."

I look at Frances, grateful for the kind things she's saying. I want to believe her, but I know that's just a fairytale fantasy.

But then I remember how gentle he was when my heel broke. I shiver as I recall his powerful fingers sliding up my leg and tickling behind my knee. With my dress covering his hands, it was a powerfully intimate and unexpectedly private moment between us. In a crowded ballroom, it was our secret.

"But you enjoyed yourself, right?" Hope fills Frances' eyes when she looks at me. She's always been my biggest cheerleader.

"Yeah, I did," I sigh. At least Frances took a picture of me before I went to the ball, so I'll be able to remind myself of the dress and shoes. "I got to feel like a princess tonight, no small thanks to you for tailoring this dress for me! Thank you so much for doing this!" I wrap my arms around Frances and hug her fiercely. She hasn't said so, but I know she'll get in trouble for doing this. Mimi is famously is a snob about dressing any woman who isn't skinny. "I wish I could keep this dress…"

I finger the red silk, remembering how it draped against my skin. Exquisite dresses have always been out of my reach. *Maybe after I send my grandparents on the cruise, I'll save up and buy something extravagant for myself.*

"I'm so glad, Chrissy. You deserve so much happiness. He'll come around, I promise."

Could Frances be right? I'm beginning to realize that there is an intensity to how Dallas treats me. If he only saw me as a conquest, he wouldn't have tenderly massaged my ankle and made sure I was okay. He's handsome and supportive, and he makes me feel like I'm the most beautiful woman in the galaxy. Being with Dallas is magical. I can't imagine not having him in my life.

My heart races in my chest and I gasp. I think I've fallen in love.

CHAPTER 8

DALLAS

I've never had a woman run away from me before.

I've also never wanted to run after a woman the way I wanted to run after Chrissy, but one of my VPs cornered me and by the time I broke free, Chrissy was gone and her phone was turned off.

I spent the entire weekend hoping she would email me, text me, call me. As each hour and minute passed, it made me feel like a teenage boy who is helpless in front of the girl who has utterly captivated him.

Walking through the office, my heart pounds when I see her. Chrissy's carrying an armful of file folders that looks like they're going to spill everywhere.

"Let me help you."

Her eyes widen in surprise, then a smile plays across her lips. Seeing that smile makes my heart thump in my chest, knowing I haven't lost her.

"Thank you, Dallas. I'd appreciate it."

We gather no small amount of looks as I walk with her, carrying file folders. In her office, I put the files on her desk and push her door closed. I don't care if people talk. I don't normally spend time in the offices of my employees…but Chrissy is so much more than an employee. I would follow her anywhere, just to be close to her. When she's in my arms, I'll protect her from everyone and everything.

"You don't have to stay." Chrissy is suddenly shy, but there's something else going on. When she looks at me, her eyes are filled with as much desire as I feel, but something holds her back. She always holds back with me, but I want her to give me everything.

"What I really want to know, is why you hold back. It's obvious you want me as much as I want you."

Chrissy collects herself and stares at me, crossing her arms over her chest like she's trying to put distance between us. "Do you really want to know?"

My skin tingles at the challenge in her question. The look in her blue eyes makes me sure that somehow, I'm not going to like what she's about to say. I nod for her to continue.

"This is the worst job I've ever had."

This is not what I was expecting. My phone buzzes in my pocket and I ignore it, not even taking a millisecond to stop the buzzing.

"Explain, please."

"Someone is trying to reach you."

"I don't care. Now, explain." She's bold when talking to me, but I'm not going to give her a chance to run away from me again. Whatever it is that's going on, we're going to resolve it right fucking now.

"Well, it's like this." Chrissy trembles, but she maintains eye contact. As much as I know I'm not going to like what she's about to say, I admire and respect that she has the nerve to be honest with me, even if it means criticizing me. "Deena is a tyrant. I've been working here for nearly two years now and every time there is a promotion or good project available, she gives it to one of her friends. I've just finished an

MBA program online, but she treats me like my degree isn't worth anything. I'm smart and good at what I do, but she continually gives me the shit tasks and I spend most of my days in this windowless closet of an office, punching numbers in spreadsheets and doing work any temp admin could handle with their eyes closed."

I keep my mouth closed as I listen to Chrissy. "How come you didn't come talk to me?"

"You're kidding, right?" Chrissy stares and me and crosses her arms over her chest. "I wasn't sure you even knew I existed, even though Deena reports directly to you. Because you hired her, I thought she was indicative of the culture here. Besides, she never let me talk to you. My career is important to me. I thought I'd have more responsibility by now, but I've realized that Deena will never promote me because I'm not in her inner circle."

"That," I say, pushing down a wave of anger at Deena, "was her doing, not mine. I thought it was well known that I have an open-door policy." This is true. I'm not going to engage in chatty conversations with employees for the kicks, but I am always available if someone has an idea or a concern. Unequivocally.

"Wait. Back up a minute." The look in Chrissy's eyes is fierce and it's sexy how passionate she is about her career. "I'd been given the impression that you'd only talk to her. She's aggressively possessive about you."

I sigh, nodding my head. To hear this about Deena isn't a surprise, because I know she's driven and it's no secret that she would love an intimate relationship with me. What *is* a surprise is how she has intentionally cut off access between me and employees who want to talk to me directly. This is unacceptable.

"That's the long and short of it. To be truthful," she says, a look of embarrassment flashing across her eyes, "I've accepted a job at King Technical Ventures. I haven't told Deena yet, but I will next week, before the new year." For the first time, she looks truly nervous.

"How come you're staying until then? You seem pretty determined to leave." It takes every fiber of my being to control my emotions. The revelation about Deena isn't much of a revelation, but I hadn't realized just how far she was pushing things.

At this, she turns her eyes back to me, jutting out her chin. "It's for my grandparents. It's their fiftieth wedding anniversary on Valentine's Day. My grandmother has always wanted to go to Hawaii, so I'm using my holiday bonus to help pay for a trip for them."

"We pay you more than that."

"Yes, you do. But I also have a student loan I'll be paying off until I'm in my grave. There isn't much left over for anything after my bills are paid. I've had to cut a lot of corners to save up for this trip for my grandparents. But it's totally worth it – family is everything to me."

Chrissy's eyes close for a long moment and the weight of her emotions hits me like a truck. This isn't the kind of company I want associated with my name. I've always considered this company my family, even if I didn't know everyone's name. It's always been important to me to have a good management team and to have happy employees.

"Don't quit. What can I do to make you stay? You can have whatever job you want."

Chrissy's pretty mouth forms a perfect "O" and I want to kiss her more than anything else in the world. She's smart and gorgeous, and she tells me it like it is. She's perfect.

"Are you saying that I could have Deena's job?" she asks, a smile quirking at the corner of her mouth.

I smile at the challenge in her eyes. She could ask to be a VP and I'd agree. "Yes, you can. Do you want it?"

S.I.L.F. (SANTA I'D LIKE TO F*)

"Of course I do! I have so many ideas!" Chrissy's blue eyes are bright and full of excitement, and I recognize the hunger for success in them. It reminds me of how I was when I started.

"Then it's settled. The job is yours." I don't even have to think twice about this decision.

"Wait." Chrissy takes a step back and levels her gaze at me, a new seriousness on her face. "Why are you doing this for me?"

"Chrissy, I believe in you. You may think I didn't know you existed before we went to The Maxwell Arms, but that's not true. There's no way I couldn't have noticed you when you joined Deena's team. If I had realized you were only doing such grunt work, I would have stepped in long ago, especially if I knew you were studying for an MBA. You deserve this level of responsibility." I pause and let Chrissy absorb this. "When I was young, a mentor took a chance on me by believing in me and giving me the chance of a lifetime. I recognize the hunger in you and I believe in you. You've earned this."

"What would happen to Deena?"

"Does it matter?" It's admirable that she thinks of other people, but it's time for Chrissy to take charge and claim what should be hers.

Chrissy's eyes are shining now and excitement is rolling off her in waves. Her fingers find my hand and squeeze tightly. I don't even know if she realizes what she's doing, but I never want her to stop. She has no idea how happy she makes me.

"Not really. I want the promotion and leadership of my own team. I want the chance to show you what I can really do. To be frank, it's a waste to have me printing reports and maintaining spreadsheets."

"Then take the job. I will also pay for your grandparent's trip to Hawaii."

"No, that's too much," Chrissy protests, but I can see the yearning in her eyes. "This is my gift to them. It's personal."

I look at her for a long moment. Perhaps there is another way.

"Consider it a signing bonus. You'll have more than enough to send your grandparents on a truly memorable trip. Is that satisfactory?"

Chrissy gives me a long look, and then she nods.

"Thank you, Dallas. This means more than you can imagine. My grandparents practically raised me and they sacrificed a lot. For most of my life, they were the only people who believed in me and supported me. Giving them this trip, while they're still healthy, is incredibly meaningful to me. I've wanted to give them a gift that conveys how much I appreciate what they did for me."

"It's a very thoughtful gift. It's meaningful to me to help you to achieve this dream of yours. All I want to do is support you. I believe in you, too. Now," I say, pulling her against my body, relishing the feel of her gorgeous curves, "we need to seal this new deal."

I give her a long, hard kiss. After a moment of surprise, she relaxes into my embrace and wraps her arms around my waist, pulling me closer. Her tongue teases mine and I groan as I grind my body against hers.

"Why did you stop?" Chrissy is breathless as I pull away from her. The air is charged with eroticism and nothing will stop me from claiming her now. I'm going to love her forever, but right now, I'm going to love every inch of her fantastically curvy body.

"It's not because I wanted to. Let's get out of here."

CHAPTER 9

CHRISSY

"This is the most amazing place I've ever seen!"

It's impossible to hide how impressed I am with Dallas' breathtaking home. It takes up the entire top floor of one of the tallest buildings in the city. The city below is a web of starry lights and the sound of traffic is faint. Inside his home, everything is sleek and beautiful, with some of the most gorgeous art I've ever seen.

"If I can tear your attention away from my art," Dallas teases when I can't stop staring at a bold abstract painting.

"It's just so beautiful…"

"It's not as beautiful as you, Chrissy."

I look at Dallas and my heart swells with love. I realize now how much he loves me and it would be impossible for me to be happier than I am right now. He believes in me and that means more to me than anything.

"I have something for you," Dallas says, gently turning me so that we're facing each other, and then kissing me deeply.

I wrap my arms around him and hold him tightly. Pure love flows through me, lighting up my heart and soul in ways

I didn't realize were possible. Now that I've tasted what love feels like, I never want to let Dallas go.

"Really?"

"Well, it is Christmas, so I have a gift for you." Dallas kisses me again and we walk across his home, stopping in front of a majestic Christmas tree.

"That's some tree you have. I wouldn't have guessed that for you." The scent of the tree makes me think of love and family. This tree is massive, but it's the kind of tree that is meant to have a large family around it, joking and passing presents and celebrating Christmas. Beneath it, there are a ton of beautifully wrapped boxes with elaborate ribbons and bows on them.

"I think you should start with this one," Dallas says, picking up one of the boxes.

"You really bought me a present?" I meet his eyes, not quite believing how lucky I am. If I'd quit this job when I originally wanted to, I would have missed discovering the love of my life.

"These are all for you," he smiles. "Consider me a not-so-secret Santa. But start with this one."

Butterflies fill my stomach when he hands me the box. It almost looks too perfect to unwrap, but excitement and curiosity get the better of me.

Removing a fancy shoe box, I gasp as I see the fancy script on the top. "Are these really...?"

"They are. It was obvious how much you loved those heels, so I bought you a new pair. In fact," he gestures back to the tree, "I bought you every style they had in stock."

Dallas kneels in front of me and slides off my work shoes, replacing them with the fancy Louboutin heels and gently kissing the tops of my feet.

"These are so beautiful and amazing! Thank you so much, Dallas! I don't know what to say." Joy rushes through my

S.I.L.F. (SANTA I'D LIKE TO F*)

body. I've never received such an extravagant gift, much less the dozens of shoes that must be in all those boxes under the tree! I've never had a man make me feel this loved in my life.

"Just say you'll be mine." Dallas stands in front of me, his voice trembles as his green eyes meet mine. He looks like he thinks he's not enough for me. His voice is vulnerable as he continues. "I love you, Chrissy. I can't envision a life without you. With all my heart and soul, I love you, and I will love you for all eternity."

"Oh, Dallas…" I reach up and put my hands on his strong jaw, my eyes filling with tears of happiness. "I love you, too. I never thought I'd find someone like you."

"Let me show you how much I love you." Dallas tenderly unzips my dress and I step out of it. "Keep the shoes on."

Dallas takes my hand and leads me to a floor-to-ceiling window that overlooks the city. He stands behind me, his hands on my hips, his body hot and hard against mine. I press my body against his, unable to help myself from grinding against him. A carnal fire burns deeply inside of me. I need to make love with Dallas, to finish what we keep starting.

"No," Dallas says, stopping me when I try to turn to face him. "Watch the city. Just feel."

I look at his reflection in the window, biting my lip in anticipation as his hands move down my body. The distant sound of a horn blaring makes me jump, but Dallas just pushes his body against mine.

"I got you," he says into my ear, his voice heavy. "You'll always be safe with me."

I lean back into Dallas and his hands are hot on my skin. I'm exposed in front of the window and it's the most thrilling thing I've ever experienced. *What if someone sees me?* It's a wicked feeling, but we're up higher than any of the other buildings. Dallas presses his fingers against the tender skin just above my mound and I shiver. When his fingers slide down and find my hot, slick core, it feels like I'm welcoming him home.

Dallas kisses the back of my neck as his fingers tease my clit. I moan as he trails kisses down my back, lingering at the top of my ass, and then moving down to my hot, slick core. I brace my hands on the window and grind my ass against him. Dallas slides his tongue through my slick slit and my moan echoes in his bedroom. I've never felt so much desire – or felt so desired – as I do right now. It's like something primal has taken over me, that I need to claim Dallas for my own and give myself to him in a way I've never wanted to give myself to anyone. I know that with Dallas, everything is special. I'll never feel this way with anyone else.

"Oh, Dallas," I moan as his tongue deliciously teases my clit and pushes me closer and closer to coming. Every lick and suck are like fireworks going off in my body. "I need you. I need to feel you inside me. Please."

"Come for me, baby. Come for me."

"Oh my God! Oh my God!"

Dallas sucks my clit faster and I bear down on his face, pleasure racing and burning in my body, and building for an explosive release. My body presses against the glass window and I gasp at the sensation of the cold glass against my feverish skin. The speed of Dallas' tongue increases and bright white spots flash in front of my eyes. My body bucks, electrified as I explode into a million shards of blinding pleasure.

My knees buckle and I grasp at the window, trying to steady myself, suddenly scared I'm going to fall.

"Oh my God." My voice is a jagged cry and for a moment life moves in slow motion.

"I've got you." Dallas turns me so that we're facing each

S.I.L.F. (SANTA I'D LIKE TO F*)

other and I wrap my arms around him. I kiss him with all my heart, loving the taste of me on his lips.

I open my eyes and see Dallas' reflection in the window, his eyes fierce and intent as they watch me. They also hold a staggering tenderness in them and in that moment, I realize he loves me. I can see how invested he is in making me happy and it moves me in a way that I've never experienced before. I know this is real, that it's forever. His fingers continue to slide through my hot wetness, but his movements are slower now.

"I want you to come, too." My skin tingles from my orgasm, but I want to push everything further. I want Dallas to feel as good as he's making me feel. "Take me to bed."

A sound like a growl comes from Dallas and my desire for him heightens.

We quickly make our way toward his bedroom. I slip out of my red-soled heels and crawl into bed, watching impatiently as Dallas strips off his clothes. I bite my lip when I see how chiseled his muscles are and how stunning his body is. Being with Dallas feels like winning the ultimate grand prize in the lottery of love.

Dallas gets into bed with me and there is an immediate urgency between us. Our mouths meet and we kiss passionately, the hot skin of our bodies burning up the sheets on his bed.

I reach down and wrap my fingers around his thick, hard cock, smiling as Dallas shudders and closes his eyes when I stroke him.

"You're all I want for Christmas," I say, straddling Dallas' waist and rubbing my hot, wet core on his cock. My eyes flutter in pleasure and I reach down to guide his long, thick shaft into me.

"Oh, Dallas." I moan his name as I lower myself onto him, my eyes fluttering from pleasure as I welcome him inside me.

We lace our fingers together and I stare into his green eyes as I rock my hips and take him deeper. He sinks a little deeper with every movement and every stroke tickles up against my g-spot, making me groan.

"You are so beautiful." Dallas' voice is thick and deep as he pulls me down to him and takes one of my breasts in his mouth, sucking hard on my nipple. My body bucks and bears down on him, moving faster and faster as we make love.

Dallas looks up at me, pure vulnerable emotion in his eyes. In that moment, I know he's sharing a part of him that he's never shared with anyone else. My hips move faster and he holds me tightly in his arms so that we are chest to chest and mouth to mouth.

"I'm going to explode," I moan into his mouth, our tongues tangling with a fierce intensity. Never in my life have I felt so connected to another person. I feel like I'm becoming something greater than myself, something new with Dallas.

Our bodies move faster and faster and in a blinding flash my body explodes. I continue to ride him as my orgasm slams into me, making me cry from happiness.

"I love you, Chrissy!" Dallas cries out as he grips my hips and slams himself up into me. His body shakes and then slowly stills, his eyes filled with love.

"I love you, too, Dallas." I kiss him as I move to his side, so that we're facing each other.

The room seems suddenly quiet, and I realize how loud I was. His fingers trace my skin and for the first time in my life, I'm completely at ease with all my curves. Dallas has made me feel truly beautiful, as if he sees what no one else ever has.

"What are you doing for Christmas?" Dallas' voice is rich and content, and he pulls my body closer to his, our faces nearly touching.

S.I.L.F. (SANTA I'D LIKE TO F*)

I snuggle into his arms. Being with him like this makes my body and soul sparkle with happiness. "I'll be visiting my grandparents. And, well," I pause, feeling a blush creep up on me, "it's also my birthday."

"What?" Dallas moves so that he can see me better. "Christmas is your *birthday*?"

"Um, yeah. That's how I have the name Christmas."

"What?"

When I see the surprise and disbelief on Dallas' face, I giggle uncontrollably. People usually make fun of me, but there's something about his reaction that just tickles me to no end.

"Yeah, I don't go around broadcasting it because everyone thinks they have a joke I haven't heard," I sigh, stifling a cringe at all the stupid jokes I've heard over the years. "My parents thought they were being clever or funny, I think. I never got a chance to ask them. Unless someone sees my driver's license, I don't tend to tell them."

"Well, my darling Christmas, Christmas just officially became my favorite person and day of the year."

Dallas pulls me close again and kisses me slowly, making my body yearn with even more desire and love for him.

"Come with me to Christmas dinner with my Grandparents. I want you to come with me," I say before I can stop myself. I know that this is moving so fast, but when you know, you *know*.

Dallas chuckles and arches his eyebrow at me. "Come with you? Again? I thought Christmas only came once a year."

I roll my eyes as I laugh and playfully swat at his arm.

"I'll have you know," I say, pausing to kiss him as I reach for his cock, "that I've already come twice tonight. And if I'm Christmas, that means you're Santa and," I grin as he hardens in my hand and groans, "if you're Santa, then you're my S.I.L.F."

"What?"

"You're my Santa I'd Like to Fuck."

Dallas laughs so loudly that tears stream from his eyes.

"That settles it. I will always be your Santa and you can always fuck me. Now hold on, because you'll never just come once a year or once a night, ever again. Christmas is going to come every night of the year."

EPILOGUE

"You could have said no to tonight, you know." I snuggle into Dallas' arms as our driver takes us home. We've just had a sumptuous dinner with my grandparents.

"Why would I say no to dinner with your grandparents?" A look of confusion passes across his eyes and once again, I don't realize how I was so lucky to meet and fall in love with Dallas. "They're important to you, so of course I make time when they invite us to dinner."

My whole life, I've never had a man take this much interest in me, much less my family, too. I always knew that life with a good man would be different and better, but I didn't realize how emotionally complete it would be.

I finger the diamond engagement ring that I'm still getting used to. For New Year's, Dallas took me to the Caribbean and we sailed around on a megayacht for a week. We spent the entire time making love and snorkeling. On the final night, he had the crew set up a special dinner on the top deck, and then he proposed to me as we watched a shooting star streak across the sky.

"I love you so much, Dallas." A heady emotional cocktail hits me. I've been able to hide them recently, but right now, I can't. Tears stream down my face and I'm on the verge of ugly-crying – all because I'm *happy*!

"Chrissy," Dallas says, moving so that he's kneeling in front of me. His voice is soft, but he can't hide the fear and tension in it. "What's wrong? Has something happened?"

I shake my head at Dallas. Breathing deeply, I look into his green eyes and it feels like I'm the only person in the world that matters. It still takes my breath away how much he loves me.

"I'm okay, my love. Really I am." I place my hands on his jaw and he leans into my hands, his eyes never leaving mine. I take a deep breath. I've been dying to tell Dallas, but I had to be sure. My emotions have been a wild rollercoaster lately. "The thing is…I'm pregnant. The doctor confirmed it this morning. I've been having wild emotional swings lately and I suspected this might be the case."

Dallas looks at me and his mouth falls open, then he gets up on his knees so that we're face to face. His mouth falls on mine and he kisses me with a passion that makes me fall in love with him even more. I run my fingers through his dark hair as every nerve ending in my body lights up like the shooting star we saw the night that he proposed to me.

When we end our kiss, we're both breathless. His eyes are bright as they look at me, and then he gently places his hands on my stomach.

"I noticed that you weren't drinking very much."

"I've been wanting to tell you all night." I run my hands through Dallas's hair and kiss him again, this time more slowly.

"Why didn't you say anything at dinner? Your grandparents will be thrilled."

S.I.L.F. (SANTA I'D LIKE TO F*)

"I wanted to tell you first." My voice catches in my throat as another wave of emotions cascades over me.

"Oh, Chrissy." A tear falls from Dallas's eye and he hugs me close to him. He reaches over to the console and pushes the button for the limo's privacy screen. I smile as I feel him unzip my dress. I can't help giggling as he pulls my dress over my shoulders and down to my waist.

"This feels kind of dangerous..." I look at Dallas, feeling even more love than I thought was possible. The love and awe in Dallas' eyes are fierce.

"You have made me the happiest man in the world, Chrissy." Dallas leans down and kisses my stomach, his fingers urging me to lift my hips. He hooks his fingers in my panties and pulls them down. "I can't wait – I have to touch you, to taste you."

I lean back in the seat, my breath jagged as he puts my legs over his shoulders and runs his tongue up the inside of my thigh and up to my hot slit. My body instinctively pushes down to his tongue, my sex hungry for attention.

Dallas's tongue finds my clit and pleasure lights up my body. I groan as he pushes three fingers inside of me, filling my tight walls and stroking my g-spot as he licks and sucks at my clit.

"Oh, Dallas," I moan, my body shaking as I look down and we meet eyes. Watching him eat me out turns me on even more and I reach up and pull my bra down so I can squeeze my nipples.

Every lick of his tongue sends me closer to coming and I grind down, my orgasm tightly building inside of me. Dallas works his fingers deep inside me and sucks hard on my clit and then my orgasm releases and flows out of me, Dallas' mouth and tongue still on my clit and making me come harder than I ever have before.

My eyes squeeze shut as my body clenches and releases

my orgasm, and my heart races.

"Kiss me." My voice is uneven as I look at Dallas. I love tasting my juices on his lips and he loves that I love this.

Dallas sits back down on the bench seat and I straddle his lap, hungrily lowering my mouth to his and licking my juices off him. He quickly unbuckles and lowers his pants just enough so that I can reach down and stroke his hard cock, and position it so I can slide down his thick shaft.

A new, deeper pleasure engulfs me as his cock drives deep inside of me and fills me up utterly.

"You are the sexiest woman in the world." Dallas' voice is jagged as I work my hips over him urgently. "I don't know how you have this effect on me…" Dallas' eyes roll up into his head as I take his thick shaft fully, "but don't ever stop. There aren't words for how much I love you."

∽

Thank you so much for reading "S.I.L.F."!
If you enjoyed this book, please leave a review on
Amazon, Goodreads, or Bookbub. Thank you!!

WANT MORE FILTY & DIRTY CHRISTMAS STORIES?
Read the full series!
https://www.amazon.com/dp/B09HMQ6TYR

Want receive updates on new books and sales? Sign up for
my mailing list!
http://eepurl.com/dh59Xr

Also by Lana Love

FOR EVEN MORE BOOKS BY Lana Love, please visit:
https://www.amazon.com/Lana-Love/e/B078KKRB1T/

Printed in Great Britain
by Amazon